LIZARD MAN

David James Poissant

Winner of the 2011 RopeWalk Press Editor's Prize

RopeWalk Press is a non-profit literary organization.

Acknowledgement is gratefully made to the following publications
in which "Lizard Man" originally appeared: *Playboy* (winner of the
Playboy College Fiction Contest), *New Stories from the South 2008*,
and *Best New American Voices 2010*. "Lizard Man" was named a
Distinguished Mystery Story of 2007 in *Best American Mystery
Stories*.

Editor: Nicole Louise Reid
Cover Art: Emily A. Reiter
Layout and Design: Nicole Louise Reid and Zach Weigand

Author inquiries and mail orders:

RopeWalk Press
College of Liberal Arts
University of Southern Indiana
8600 University Boulevard
Evansville, IN 47712
ropewalkpress@usi.edu
ropewalk.org

for Jonathan Jones

LIZARD MAN

I rattle into the driveway around sunup and Cam's on my front stoop with his boy, Bobby. Cam stands. He's a huge man, thick and muscled from a decade of work in construction. Sleeves of green dragons run armpit to wrist. He claims there's a pair of naked ladies tattooed into all those scales if you look close enough.

When Crystal left him, Cam got the boy, which tells you what kind of a mother Crystal was. Cam's my last friend. He's a saint when he's sober, and he hasn't touched liquor in ten years.

He puts a hand on the boy's shoulder, but Bobby spins from his grip and charges. He meets me at the truck, grabs my leg and hugs it with his whole body. I head toward Cam. Bobby bounces and laughs with every step.

We shake hands, but Cam's expression is no-nonsense.

"Graveyard again?" he says. My apron, rolled into a tan tube, hangs from my front pocket and I reek of kitchen grease.

"Yeah," I say. I haven't told Cam how I lost my temper and yelled at a customer, how apparently some people don't know what *over easy* means, how my agreement to work the ten-to-six shift is the only thing keeping my electricity on and the water running.

"Bobby," Cam says, "go play for a minute, OK?" Bobby releases my leg and stares at his father skeptically. "Don't make me tell you twice," Cam says. The boy runs to my mailbox, drops to the lawn, cross-legged, and scowls. "Keep going," Cam says. Slowly, deliberately, Bobby stands and sulks toward their house.

"What is it?" I say. "What's wrong?"

Cam shakes his head. "Red's dead," he says.

Red is Cam's dad. "Bastard used to beat the fuck out of me," Cam said one night back when we both drank too much and swapped sad stories. When he turned 18, Cam enlisted and left for the first Gulf War. The last time he saw his father, the man was staggering, drunk, across the lawn. "Go then!" he screamed. "Go die for your fucking country!" Bobby never knew he had a grandfather.

I don't know whether Cam is upset or relieved, and I don't know what to say. Cam must see this because he says: "It's OK. I'm OK."

"How'd it happen?" I ask.

"He was drinking," Cam says. "Bartender said one minute Red was laughing, the next his forehead was on the bar. When they went to shake him awake, he was dead.

"Wow." It's a stupid thing to say, but I've been up all night. My hand still grips an invisible steel spatula. I can feel lard under my nails.

"I need a favor," Cam says.

"Anything," I say. When I was in jail, it was Cam who bailed me out. When my wife and son moved to Baton Rouge, it was Cam who knocked down my door, kicked my ass, threw the contents of my liquor cabinet onto the front lawn, set it on fire, and got me a job at his friend's diner.

"I need a ride to Red's house," Cam says.

"OK," I say. Cam hasn't had a car for years. Half the people on our block can't afford storm shutters, let alone cars, but it's St. Petersburg, a pedestrian city, and downtown's only a five-minute walk.

"Well, don't say OK yet," Cam says. "It's in Lee."

"Lee, Florida?"

Cam nods. Lee is four hours north, the last city you pass on I-75 before you hit Georgia.

"No problem," I say, "as long as I'm back before ten tonight."

"Another graveyard?" Cam asks. I nod. "OK," he says, "let's go."

~

Last year, I threw my son through the family room window. I don't remember how it happened, not exactly. I remember stepping into the room. I remember seeing Jack, his mouth pressed to the mouth of the other boy, his hands moving fast in the boy's lap. Then I stood over him in the garden. Lynn ran from the house, screaming. She saw Jack and hit me in the face.

She battered my shoulders and my chest. Above us, through the window frame, the other boy stood, staring, shaking, hugging himself with his thin arms. Jack lay on the ground. He did not move except for the rise and fall of his chest. The window had broken cleanly and there was no blood, just shards of glass scattered over flowers, but one of Jack's arms was bent behind his head, as though he had gone to sleep that way, an elbow for a pillow.

"Call 911," Lynn yelled to the boy above.

"No," I said. Whatever else I didn't know in that time and place, I knew we could never afford an ambulance ride. "I'll take him," I said.

"No!" Lynn cried. "You'll kill him!"

"I'm not going to kill him," I said. "Come here." I gestured to the boy. He shook his head and stepped back. "Please," I said.

Tentatively, the boy stepped over the jagged edge of the sill. He planted his feet on the brick ledge of the front wall, then dropped the few feet to the ground. Glass crunched beneath his sneakers.

"Grab his ankles," I said. I hooked my hands under Jack's armpits and we lifted him. One arm trailed the ground as we walked him to the car. Lynn opened the hatchback. We laid Jack in the back and covered him with a blanket. It seemed like the right thing, what you see on TV.

A few neighbors had come outside to watch. We ignored them.

"I'll need you with me," I said to the boy. "When we're done, I'll take you home." The boy was wringing the hem of his shirt in both hands. His eyes brimmed with tears. "I won't hurt you, if that's what you think."

We set off for the hospital, Lynn following in my pickup. The boy sat beside me in the passenger seat, his body pressed to the door, face against the window, the seatbelt strap clenched in one hand at his waist. With each bump in the road, he turned to look at Jack.

"What's your name?" I asked.

"Alan," he said.

"How old are you, Alan?"

"Seventeen."

"Seventeen. Seventeen. And have you ever been with a woman, Alan?"

Alan looked at me. His face drained of color. His hand tightened on the seatbelt.

"It's a simple question, Alan. I'm asking you: Have you been with a woman?"

"No," Alan said. "No, sir."

"Then how do you know you're gay?"

In back, Jack began to stir. He moaned, then grew silent. Alan watched him.

"Look at me, Alan," I said. "I asked you a question. If you've never been with a woman, then how do you know you're gay?"

"I don't know," Alan said.

"You mean, you don't know that you're gay, or you don't know how you know?"

"I don't know how I know," Alan said. "I just do."

We passed the bakery, the Laundromat, the supermarket, and entered the city limits. In the distance, the silhouette of the helicopter on the hospital's roof. Behind us, the steady pursuit of the pickup truck.

"And your parents, do they know about this?" I asked.

"Yes," Alan said.

"And do they approve?"

"Not really."

"No. I bet they don't, Alan. I'll bet they do not."

I glanced in the rearview mirror. Jack had not opened his eyes, but he had a hand to his temple. The other hand, the one attached to the broken arm, lay at his side. The fingers moved, but without purpose, the hand spasming from fist to open palm.

"I just have one more question for you, Alan," I said.

Alan looked like he might be sick. He watched the road unfurl before us. He was afraid of me, afraid to look at Jack.

"What right do you have teaching my son to be gay?"

"I didn't!" Alan said. "I'm not!"

"You're not? Then what do you call that? Back there? That business on the couch?"

"Mr. Lawson," Alan said, and, here, the tone of his voice changed, and I felt as though I were speaking to another man. "With all due respect, sir, Jack came on to me."

"Jack is not gay."

"He is. I know it. Jack knows it. Your *wife* knows it. I don't know how you couldn't know it. I don't see how you've missed the signals."

I tried to imagine what signals, but I couldn't. I couldn't recall a thing that would have signaled that I'd wind up here, delivering my son to the hospital with a concussion and a broken arm. What signal might have foretold that, following this day, after two months spent in a motel and two months in prison, my wife of twenty years would divorce me because, as she put it, I was *full of hate*?

I pulled up to the emergency room's entryway and Alan helped me pull Jack from the car. A nurse with a wheelchair ran out to meet us. We settled Jack into the chair and she wheeled him away.

I pulled the car into a parking spot and walked back to the entrance. Alan stood on the curb where I had left him.

"Where's Lynn?" I said.

"Inside," Alan said. "Jack's awake."

"All right, I'm going in. I suggest you get out of here."

"But, you said you'd drive me home."

"Sorry," I said. "I changed my mind."

Alan stared at me, dumbfounded. His hands groped the air.

"Hey," I said, "I got a signal for you." I gave him a hitchhiker's thumb's up and cast it over my shoulder as I entered the hospital.

~

I wake and Cam's making his way down back roads, their surfaces cratered with potholes.

"Rise and shine," he says, "and welcome to Lee."

It's nearly noon. The sun is bright and the cab is hot. I wipe gunk from my eyes and drool from the corner of my mouth. Cam watches the road with one eye and studies directions he's scrawled in black ink across the back of a cereal box. He's never seen the house where his father spent his last twenty years.

We turn onto a dirt road. The truck lurches into and then out of an enormous, waterlogged hole. Pines line the road. Their needles shiver as we go by. We pass turn after turn, but only half of the roads are marked. Every few miles, we pass a driveway, the house deep in the trees and out of sight. It's a haunted place and I'm already ready to leave.

Cam says, "I don't know where the fuck we are."

We drive some more. I think about Bobby home alone, how Cam gave him six VHS tapes. "By the time you watch all of these," he said, "I'll be back." Then he put in the first movie, something Disney, and we left. "He'll be fine," Cam said. "He'll never even know we're gone."

"We could bring him with us," I said, but Cam had refused.

"There's no telling what we'll find there," he said.

Ahead, a child stands beside the road. Cam slows the truck to a halt and rolls down the window. The girl steps forward. She looks over her shoulder, then back at us. She is barefoot and her face is smeared with dirt. She wears a brown dress and a green bow in her hair. A string is looped around her wrist and from the end of the string floats a blue balloon.

"Hi there," Cam says. He leans out the window, his hand extended, but the child does not take it. Instead, she stares at his arms, the coiled dragons. She takes a step back.

"You're scaring her," I say.

Cam glares at me, but he returns his head to the cab and his hand to the wheel and gives the girl his warmest smile. "Do you know where we could find Cherry Road?" he says.

"Sure," the girl says. She pumps her arm and the balloon bobs in response. "It's that way," she says, pointing in the direction from which we've come.

"About how far?" Cam asks.

"Not the next road but the next. But it's a dead end. There's only one house." She flails her wrist and the balloon thunks against her fist.

Cam glances at the cereal box. "That's the one," he says.

"Oh," the girl says, and for a moment she is silent. "You're going to visit the Lizard Man. I seen him. I seen him once."

Cam looks at me. I shrug. We look at the girl.

"Well, thank you," Cam says. The girl gives the balloon a good shake. Cam turns the truck around and the girl waves goodbye.

"Cute kid," I say. We turn onto Cherry.

"Creepy little fucker," Cam says.

~

The house is hidden in pines and the yard is overgrown with knee-high weeds. Tire tracks mark where the driveway used to be. Plastic flamingos dot the yard, their curved beaks peeking out of the weeds, wire legs rusted, bodies bleached a light pink.

The roof of the house is littered with pine needles and piles of shingles where someone abandoned a roofing project. The porch has buckled and the siding is rotten, the planks loose. I press a fingernail to the soft wood and it slides in.

Our mission is unclear. There's no body to ID or papers to sign. Nothing to inherit, and there will be no funeral. But I know why we're here. This is how Cam will say goodbye.

The front door is locked but gives with two kicks. "Right here," Cam says. He taps the wood a foot above the lock before slamming the heel of his boot through the door.

Inside, the house waits for its owner's return. The hallway light is on. The AC unit shakes in the window over the kitchen sink. Tan wallpaper curls away from the cabinets like birch bark exposing thin ribbons of yellow glue on the walls.

We hear voices. Cam puts a hand to my chest and a finger to his lips. He brings a hand to his waist and feels for a gun that is not there. Neither of us moves for a full minute, then Cam laughs.

"Fuck!" he says. "That's a TV." He hoots. He runs a hand through his hair. "About scared the shit out of me."

We move to the main room. It, too, is in disarray, the lampshades thick with dust, a coffee table awash in a sea of newspapers and unopened mail. There is an old and scary looking couch, its arms held to its sides with duct tape. A pair of springs pokes through the cushion, ripe with tetanus.

The exception is the television. It is beautiful. It is six feet of widescreen glory. "Look at that picture," I say, and Cam and I step back to take it in. The TV's tuned to the Military Channel, some cable extravagance. B-2 Bombers streak the sky in black and white, propellers the size of my head. On top of the set sits a bottle of Windex and a filthy washcloth along with several many-buttoned remote controls. Cam grabs one, fondles it, holds down a button, and the sound swells. The drone of plane engines and firefight tear across the room from one speaker to another. I jump. Cam grins.

"We're taking it," he says. "We are so taking this shit."

He pushes another button and the picture blips to a single point of white at the center of the screen. The point fades and dies.

"No!" Cam says. "No!"

"What did you do?" I say.

"I don't know. I don't know!"

Cam shakes the remote, picks up another, punches more buttons, picks up a third, presses its buttons. The television hums and the picture shimmers back to life.

"Ahhh," Cam says. We sit, careful to avoid the springs. While we watch, the beaches at Normandy are stormed, two bombs are dropped, and the war is won. We're halfway into Vietnam when Cam says, "I'm going to check out his room." It is not an invitation.

Cam's gone for half an hour. When he returns, he looks terrible. The color is gone from his face and his eyes are red-rimmed. He carries a shoebox under one arm. I don't ask and he doesn't offer.

"Let's load up the set and get out of here," Cam says. "I'll pull the truck around."

I hear a glass door slide open then shut behind me. I hear something like a scream. Then the door slides open again. I turn around to see Cam. If he looked bad before, now he looks downright awful.

"What is it?" I say.

"Big," Cam says. "In the backyard."

"What? What's big in the backyard?"

"Big. Fucking. Alligator."

~

It *is* a big fucking alligator. I've seen alligators before, in movies, at zoos, but never this big and never so close. We stare at him. We don't know it's a *him*, but we decide it's a *him*. He is big. It's insane.

It's also the saddest fucking thing I have ever seen. In the backyard is a makeshift cage, an oval of chain link fence with a chicken wire roof. Inside, the alligator straddles an old kiddie pool. The pool's cracked plastic lip strains with the alligator's weight. His middle fills the pool, his belly submerged in a few inches of syrupy brown water, legs hanging out. His tail, the span of a man, curls against a length of chain link.

When he sees us, the alligator hisses and paddles his front feet in the air. He opens his jaws, baring yellow teeth and white, fleshy gums. Everywhere there are flies and gnats. They fly into his open mouth and land on his teeth. Others swarm open wounds along his back.

"What is he doing here?" Cam asks.

"Red was the Lizard Man," I say. "Apparently."

We stare at the alligator. He stares back. I consider the cage and wonder whether the alligator can turn around.

"He looks bored," Cam says. And it's true. He looks bored, and sick. He shuts his mouth and his open eyes are the only thing reminding me he's alive.

"We can't leave him here," Cam says.

"We should call someone," I say. But who would we call? The authorities? Animal control?

"We can't," Cam says. "They'll kill him."

Cam is right. I've seen it before, on the news. Some jackass raises a gator. The gator gets loose. It's been handfed and knows no fear of man. The segments always end the same way: *Sadly, the alligator had to be destroyed.*

"I don't see that we have a choice," I say.

"We have the pickup," Cam says.

My mouth says, *No*, but my eyes must say, *Yes*, because before I know what's happening, we're in the front yard examining the bed of the truck, Cam measuring the length with his open arms.

"This won't work," I say. Cam ignores me. He pulls a blue tarp from the backseat and unrolls it on the ground beside the truck.

"He'll never fit," I say.

"He'll fit. It'll be close, but he'll fit."

"Cam," I say. "Wait. Stop." Cam leans against the truck. He looks right at me. "Say we get the alligator out of the cage and into the truck. Say we manage to do this and keep all of our fingers. Where do we take him? I mean, what the hell, Cam? What the hell do you do with twelve feet of living, breathing, alligator? And what about the TV? I thought you wanted to take the TV."

"Shit. I forgot about the TV."

We stare at the truck. I look up. The sky has turned from bright to light blue and the sun has disappeared behind a scatter of clouds. On the ground, one corner of the tarp flaps in the breeze, winking its gold eyelet.

Cam bows his head, as if in mourning. "Maybe if we stand the set up on its end."

"Cam," I say. "We can take the alligator or we can take the television, but we can't take both."

~

Electric-taping the snout, Cam decides, will be the hard part.

"All of it's the hard part," I say, but Cam's not listening.

Cam finds a T-bone in Red's refrigerator. It's spoiled, but the alligator doesn't seem to mind. Cam sets the steak near the cage and the alligator waddles out of the pool. He presses his nostrils to the fence. The thick musk of alligator and reek of rotten meat turn my stomach and I retch.

"You puke, I kick your ass," Cam says.

We've raided Red's garage for supplies. Lying scattered at our feet are bolt cutters, a roll of electric tape, a spool of twine, bungee cords, a dozen two-by-fours, my tarp, and, for no reason I'm immediately able to ascertain, a chainsaw.

"Protection," Cam says, nudging the old Sears model with his toe. The chain is rusted and hangs loose from the blade. I imagine Cam starting the chainsaw, the chain snapping, flying, landing far away in the tall grass. I try to picture the struggle between man and beast, Cam pinned beneath 500 pounds of alligator, Cam's head in the gator's mouth, Cam dragged in circles around the yard, a tangle of limbs and screams. In each scenario, the chainsaw offers little assistance.

Cam's hands are sheathed in oven mitts, a compromise he accepted begrudgingly when the boxing gloves he found, while offering superior protection, failed to provide him the ability to grip, pick up, or hold.

"This is stupid," I say. "Are we really doing this?"

"We're doing this," Cam says. He swats a fly from his face with one potholdered hand.

There is a clatter of chain link. We turn to see the alligator nudging the fence with his snout. He snorts, eyes the T-bone, opens and shuts his mouth. He really is surprisingly large.

Cam's parked the pickup in the backyard. He pulls off his oven mitts, lowers the gate, exposing the wide, bare bed of the truck, and we set to work angling the two-by-fours from gate to grass. We press the planks together and Cam cinches them tight with the bungee cords. The boards are long, ten or twelve feet, so physics is on our side. We should be able to drag him up the incline.

We return our attention to the alligator who is sort of throwing himself against the fence, except that he can only back up a few feet and therefore build very little momentum. Above his head, at knee level, is a hand-sized wire mesh door held shut by a combination lock. With each lunge, the lock jumps, then clatters against the door. With each charge, I jump, too.

"He can't break out," Cam says. He picks up the bolt cutters.

"You don't know that," I say.

"If he could, don't you think he'd have done it by now?" Cam positions the bolt cutters on the loop of lock, bows his legs, and squats. He squeezes and his face reddens. He grunts, there's a snap, and the lock falls away, followed by a flash of movement. Cam howls and falls. The alligator's open jaws stretch halfway through the hole. All I see is teeth.

"Motherfucker!" Cam yells.

"You OK?" I say.

Cam holds up his hands, wiggles ten fingers.

"OK," Cam says. "OK." He picks up the T-bone and throws it at the alligator. The steak lands on his nose, hangs there, then slides off.

"It's not a dog," I say. "This isn't catch."

Cam puts on the oven mitts and slowly reaches for the meat resting in the grass just a few feet beneath all those teeth. Suddenly, the pen looks less sturdy, less like a thing the alligator could never escape.

The cage shakes, but this time it's the wind, which has really picked up. I wonder whether it's storming in St. Petersburg. Cam should be at home with Bobby, and I almost say as much. But Cam's eyes are wild. He's dead-set on doing this.

Cam says, "I'm going to put the steak into his mouth, and, when I do, I want you to tape the jaws shut."

"No way," I say. "No way am I putting my hand in range of that thing." And then this happens: My son walks out of my memory and into my thoughts, his arm hanging loose at the

elbow. The nurse asks what happened, and he looks up, ready
to lie for me. There is something beautiful in the pause between
this question and the one to come. Then there's the officer's hand
on my shoulder, the "Would you mind stepping out with me,
please?" Oh, I've heard it a hundred times. It never leaves me.
It is a whisper. It is a prison sentence.

I want to put the elbow back into the socket myself. I want
to turn back time. I want Jack at five or ten. I want him curled
in my lap like a dog. I want him writing on the walls with an
orange crayon and blaming the angels that live in the attic.
I want him before his voice plummeted two octaves, before
he learned to stand with a hand on one hip, before he grew
confused. I want my boy back.

"Come on!" Cam shouts. "Don't puss out on me now.
As soon as he bites down, just wrap the tape around it."

"Give me your oven mitts," I say.

"No!"

"Give me the mitts and I'll do it."

"But you won't be able to handle the tape."

"Trust me," I say, "I'll find a way."

We do it. Cam waves the cut of meat at the snout until it
smacks teeth. The jaws grab. There's an unnatural crunch as
the T in the T-Bone becomes two Is and then a pile of periods.
I drape a length of tape over the nose, fasten the ends beneath
the jaws, then run my gloved hands up both strands of tape,
sealing them. Then I start wrapping like crazy. I wind the roll
of tape around and around the jaws. The tape unspools from
the roll and coils in a flat, black worm around the snout.

When I step back, the alligator's jaws are shut tight and my
hands shake.

"I can't believe it," Cam says. "I can't believe you actually
did that shit."

~

The alligator's one heavy son of a bitch. We hold him in a
kind of headlock, arms cradling his neck and front legs, fingers

13

gripping his scaly hide. It's a good twenty feet from cage to truck.
We sidestep toward the pickup, the alligator's back end and tail
tracing a path through the grass. Every few feet, we stop to rest.

When we drag, the alligator's back feet scramble and claw at
the ground, but he doesn't writhe or thrash. He is not a healthy
alligator. I stop.

"C'mon," Cam says. "Almost there."

"What are we doing?" I say.

"We're putting an alligator into your truck," Cam says. "C'mon."

"But look at him," I say. Cam looks down, examines
the alligator's wide, green head, his wet, ping-pong ball eyes.
He looks up.

"No," I say. "Really look."

"What?" Cam's impatient. He shifts his weight, gets a better
grip on the gator. "I don't know what you want me to see."

"He's not even fighting us. He's too sick. Even if we set him
free, how do we know he'll make it?"

"We don't."

"No, we don't. We don't know where he came from. We don't
know where to take him. And what if Red raised him? How will
he survive in the wild? How will he learn to hunt and catch fish
and stuff?"

Cam shrugs, shakes his head.

"So, why?" I ask. "Why are we doing this?"

Cam locks eyes with me. After a minute, I look away. My arms
are weak with the weight of alligator. My legs quiver. We shuffle
forward.

~

I didn't give Jack the chance to lie. I admitted guilt to second-
degree battery and kept everyone out of court. I got four months
and served two, plus fines, plus community service. Had that been
the end of it, I'd have gotten off easy. Instead, I lost my family.

The last time I saw Jack, he stood beside his mother's car
showing Alan his new driver's license. They reclined like

girls against the hood but laughed like men at something on the license: a typo. *Weight: 1500.* I watched them from the doorway. Jack kept his distance, flinched when I came close.

Alan had helped me load the furniture. With each piece, I thought of Jack's body. How it hung between us that afternoon, how it swayed, how much like a game wherein you and a friend grab another boy by ankles and wrists and throw him off a dock and into a lake.

Everything Jack and Lynn owned we'd packed into a U-Haul truck. I was not meant to know where they were going. I was not meant to see them again, but I'd found maps and directions in a pile of Lynn's things and had written down the address of their new place in Baton Rouge. I could forgive Lynn not wanting to see me, but taking my son away was a thing I could not abide.

I decided I would go there one day, a day that seems more distant with each passing afternoon. And what would Jack do when he opened the door? In my dreams, it was always Jack who opened the door. I would open my arms in invitation. I would say what I had not said.

But that afternoon, it was Alan who sent Jack to me. Lynn waited in the U-Haul, ready to drive away. Alan gestured in my direction. He and Jack argued in hushed voices. And finally, remarkably, Jack moved toward me. I did not leave the doorway, and Jack stopped just short of the stoop.

What can I tell you about my son? He had been a beautiful boy, and, standing before me, I saw that he had become something different: A man I did not understand. His t-shirt was too tight for him and the hem rode just above his navel. A trail of light brown hair led from there and disappeared behind a silver belt buckle. His fingernails were painted black. The cast had come off, and his right arm was a nest of curly, dark hairs.

I wanted to say, "I want to understand you."

I wanted to say, "I will do whatever it takes to earn your trust."

I wanted to say, "I love you," but I had never said it, not to Jack—yes, I am one of those men—and I could not bear the thought of speaking these words to my son for the first time and not hearing them spoken in return.

Instead, I said nothing.

Jack held out his hand and we shook like strangers.

I still feel it, the infinity of Jack's handshake: The nod of pressed palms, flesh of my flesh.

~

The rain arrives in sheets and the windshield wipers can hardly keep up. I drive. Cam sits beside me. He's placed the shoebox on the seat between us. His arm rests protectively against the lid. The alligator slides around with the two-by-fours in the back. We fastened the tarp over the bed of the truck to conceal our cargo, but we didn't pull it taut. The tarp sags with water, threatening to smother the animal underneath.

Cam flips on the radio and we catch snippets of the weather before the speakers turn to static.

"...upgraded to a tropical storm...usually signals the formation of a hurricane...storm will pick up speed as it makes its way across the Gulf...expected to come ashore as far north as the panhandle... far south as St. Petersburg..."

Cam turns the radio off. We watch rain pelt the windshield, the black flash of wipers pushing water.

I don't ask whether Bobby is afraid of storms. As a boy, I'd been frightened, but not Jack. During storms, Jack had stood at the window and watched as branches skittered down the street and power lines unraveled onto the sidewalks. He smiled and stared until Lynn pulled him away from the glass and we moved to the bathroom with our blankets and flashlights. It was only then, huddled in the dark, that Jack sometimes cried.

"We should go back," I say. "The power could be out."

"Bobby's a tough kid," Cam says. "He'll be fine."

"Cam," I say.

"In case you've forgotten, there's a fucking alligator in the back of your truck."

I say nothing. Whatever happens is Cam's responsibility. *This*, I tell myself, *is not your fault.*

Thunder shakes the truck. Not far ahead, a cell tower ignites with lightning. A shower of sparks waterfalls onto the highway. Cars and trucks are dusted with fire. Everyone drives on.

I don't know where we're headed, but Cam says we're close.

Cam, I think, *after this, I owe you nothing. Once this is over, we're even.*

"If it's work you're worried about," Cam says, "I'll talk to Mickey. I'll tell him about Red. He'll understand if you're late."

"It's not Mickey I'm worried about," I say. I don't say: *Mickey can kiss my ass.* I don't say: *You and Mickey can go to hell.*

"Look," Cam says, "I know why you're pulling the graveyard shift. Mickey told me what you did. But this is different. This he'll understand."

I recognize the ache at the back of my throat immediately. The second I'm alone, it will take a miracle to keep a bottle out of my hand.

"Take this exit," Cam says. "At the bottom, turn right."

I guide the truck down the ramp toward Grove Street. The water in back sloshes forward and unfloods the tarp. Alligator feet scratch for purchase on the truck bed's corrugated plastic lining.

"Where are you taking us?" I ask.

"Havenbrook," he says. I wait for Cam to say he's kidding. But Cam isn't kidding.

~

The largest of the lakes cradles the seventeenth green. Cam's seen gators there before, big bastards who come ashore to sun themselves and scare off golfers. I've never golfed in my life, and neither has he, but Cam led the team that patched the clubhouse roof following last year's hurricane season. He remembers the five-digit code, and it still works. The security gate slides open, and we head down the paved drive reserved for maintenance.

No one's on the course. Fallen limbs litter the greens. An abandoned white cart lies turned on its side where the golf cart path rounds the fifteenth hole.

Lightning streaks the sky. The rain has turned the windshield to water and sudden gusts of wind jostle the truck from every direction. I fight the steering wheel to stay on the asphalt. Even Cam is wide-eyed, his fingers buried in the seat cushions. The shoebox bounces between us.

We reach the lake, but the shore is half a football field away. The green is soggy, thick with water, and already the lake is flooding its banks. The first tire that leaves the road, I know, will sink into the mud and we'll never get the truck out.

"I can't drive out there," I tell Cam. I have to yell over the wind and rain, the deafening thunder. It's like the world is pulling apart. "This is the closest I can get us."

Cam says something I can't hear and then he's out of the truck, the door slamming behind him. I jump out and the wet cold slaps me. Within seconds, I'm drenched, my clothes heavy. All I hear is the wind. I move as if underwater.

As soon as Cam gets the tarp off, the storm catches it and it billows into the sky like a flaming blue parachute, up into the trees overhead. It tangles itself into the branches and then there is only the *smack smack* of the tarp's uncaught corners pummeled by gusts.

Cam screams at me. His teeth flash in bursts of lightning, but his words are choked by wind. I tap my ear and he nods. He motions toward the alligator. We approach it slowly. I expect the animal to charge, but he lies motionless. I check the jaws. They're still wrapped tight. This, I realize, will be our last challenge. If he gets away from us before we remove the tape, he's doomed.

I'm wondering which of us will climb into the bed of the truck when the gator starts scuttling forward. We leap out of the way as hundreds of pounds of reptile spill from the truck and onto the green. The gate cracks under the weight and swings loose like a trapdoor in midair, the hinges busted. Then the alligator is free on the grass. We don't move and neither does he.

Cam approaches me. He makes a megaphone of his cupped hands and mouth and leans in close to my ear. His hot breath on my face is startling and sudden and wonderful in all that fierce cold and rain.

"I think he's stunned," Cam yells. "We've got to get the tape off, now."

I nod. I am exhausted and anxious and I know there's no way we'll be able to lug the alligator to the water's edge. I wonder whether he'll make it, if he'll find his way to the water, or if this fall from the truck was the final blow, if tomorrow the groundskeepers will find an alligator carcass fifty yards from the lake. It would make the front page of the *St. Petersburg Times*: GIANT ALLIGATOR KILLED IN HURRICANE. Officials would be baffled.

"I want you to straddle its neck," Cam yells. "Keep its head pressed to the ground. I'll try to get the tape off."

"No," I say. I point to my chest. I circle my hand through the air, pantomiming the unraveling. Cam looks surprised, but he nods.

Cam brings his hands to my face again and yells his hot words into my ear. "On my signal," he screams, but I push him away.

I don't wait for a signal. Before I know it, I'm on the ground, my side hugging mud, and I'm digging my nails into the tape. My eye is inches from the alligator's eye. He blinks without blinking, a thin, clear membrane sliding over his eyeball, then up and under his eyelid. It is a thing to see. It is a knowing wink. I see this and I feel safe.

The tape is harder to unwrap than it was to wrap. The rain has made it soft, the glue gooey. Every few turns, I lose my grip. Finally, I let the tape coil around my hand like a snake. It unwinds and soon my fist is a ball of dark, sticky fruit. The last of the tape pulls cleanly from the snout and I roll away from the alligator.

I stand and Cam pulls me back. He holds me up. The alligator flexes his jaws. His mouth opens wide, then slams shut. And then he's off, zigzagging toward the water.

He is swift and strong, and I'm glad it is cold and raining so Cam can't see the tears streaking my cheeks and won't know that my shivering is from sobbing. Cam lets go of me and I think I will fall, but instead I am running. Running! And I'm laughing and hollering and leaping. I'm pumping my fist into the air. I'm screaming, "Go! Go!" And, just before the alligator reaches the water, I lunge and my fingertips trace the last ridges and scales of tail whipping their way ahead of me. The sky is alive with lightning and I see the hulking body, so awkward and graceless on land, slide into the water as it was meant to do. That great body cuts the water, fast and sleek, and the alligator dives out of sight, at home in the world where he belongs, safe in the warm quiet of mud and fish and unseen things that thrive in deep, green darkness.

~

Cam and I don't say much on the ride home. The rain has slowed to an even, steady downpour. The truck's cab has grown cold. Cam holds his hands close to the vents to catch whatever weak streams of heat trickle out. We have done a good thing, Cam says, and I agree, but I worry at what cost? We listen to the radio, but the storm has headed north. The reporters have moved on to new cities: Clearwater, Crystal Springs, Ocala.

"There was this one time," Cam says at last. "About five years back. I spoke to Red."

This is news to me. This, I know, is no small revelation.

"I called him," Cam says. "I called him up, and I said, 'Dad? I just want you to know that you have a grandson and that his name is Robert and that I think he should know his grandfather.' And you know what that prick did? He hung up. The only thing Red said to me in twenty years was 'Hello' when he picked up the phone."

"I'm sorry," I say.

"If he'd even once told me he was sorry, I'd have forgiven him anything. I'd have forgiven him my own murder. He was my father. I would have forgiven everything.

"Do you know why I got all these fucking tattoos? To hide the scars from the night Red cut me with a fillet knife, and I'd have forgiven that if he'd just said something, anything, when he answered the phone."

Cam doesn't shake or sob or bang a fist on the dashboard, but, when I look away, I catch his reflection in the window, a knuckle in each eye socket, and I'm suddenly sorry for my impatience, the grudge I've carried all afternoon.

"But you tried," I say. "At least you won't spend your life wondering."

We sit in silence for a while. The rain on the roof beats a cadence into the cab and it soothes me.

"You know, I served with gay guys in the Gulf," Cam says, and I almost drive the truck off the road. A tire slips over the lip of asphalt and my side mirror nearly catches a guardrail before I bring the truck back to the center of the lane.

"Jesus!" Cam says. "I'm just saying, they were OK guys, and if Jack's gay it's not the end of the world."

"Jack's confused," I say. "He isn't gay."

"Well, either he is or he isn't, and what you think or want or say won't change it."

"Cam," I say, "all due respect. This doesn't concern you."

"I know," Cam says. He sits up straighter in his seat, grips the door handle as we pull onto our block. "I'm just saying, it isn't too late."

We pull into the driveway. Cam jumps out of the truck before it's in park. The yard is a mess of fallen limbs and garbage. Two shutters have been torn from the front of the house. The mailbox is on its side. Otherwise, everything looks all right. I glance down the street and see that my house is still standing.

When I turn back to Cam's house, what I see breaks my heart in ten places. I see Cam running across the lawn. I see Bobby, his hands pressed to the big bay window. His face is puffy and red. Cam disappears into the house, and then he is there with the boy, he is there on his knees, and he pulls Bobby to him. He mouths the words, *I'm sorry, I'm sorry,* over and over again, and Bobby collapses into him, buries his head in Cam's chest, and my friend wraps his son in dragons.

I watch them. They stay like that for minutes, framed by window and house and the darkening sky. I watch, and then I open the shoebox and look inside.

I don't know what I was expecting, but it wasn't this. What I find are letters, over a hundred of them. About a letter a month for roughly ten years, all of them unopened. Each has been dated and stamped RETURN TO SENDER, the last one sent back just a week ago. Each is marked by the same shaky handwriting. Each is addressed to a single recipient, Mr. Cameron Starnes, from a single sender: Red.

And I know then that there was no phone call, no forgiveness on Cam's part, that Cam never came close until after the monster was safely out of reach.

I stare at the letters and I know who it is Cam wants to keep me from becoming.

I pull out of Cam's driveway. I stop to right Cam's mailbox, then I tuck the shoebox safely inside. I follow the street to the end of the block. At the stop sign, I pause. I don't know whether to turn right or left. Finally, I head for the interstate. There's a spare uniform at the diner, clean and dry, and if I hurry I won't be late for work.

But I'm not going to work.

It's a ten-hour drive to Baton Rouge, but I will make it in eight. I will make it before morning. I will drive north, following the storm. I will drive through the wind and the rain. I will drive all night.

**David James Poissant's** stories have appeared in *The Atlantic, Playboy, One Story, The Southern Review, Mississippi Review, New Stories from the South, Best New American Voices,* and elsewhere. Winner of the *Playboy* College Fiction Contest, the George Garrett Fiction Award, the Matt Clark Prize, the Alice White Reeves Memorial Award from the National Society of Arts and Letters, and Second and Third Prizes in the *Atlantic Monthly* Student Writing Contest, he holds an MFA from the University of Arizona and a PhD from the University of Cincinnati. He recently joined the MFA faculty at the University of Central Florida. He lives in Orlando with his wife and daughters.

This chapbook is made possible by grants from the Indiana
Arts Council, the Arts Council of Southwestern Indiana, and the
University of Southern Indiana Society for Arts & Humanities.

The **Arts Council**
of Southwestern Indiana

Regional Arts Partner

IAC
Indiana Arts Commission

This activity made possible, in part, by the Arts
Council of Southwestern Indiana, the Indiana Arts
Commission, and the National Endowment for the
Arts, a federal agency

USI◆SOCIETY◆FOR
ARTS&HUMANITIES